THE SEVEN SEAS OF BILLY'S BATHTUB

By Ray Nelson Jr. and Douglas Kelly

For Bruce McKean

A FLYING RHINO BOOK

Flying Rhino Productions
3629 SW Caldew
Portland, Oregon 97219
Library of Congress Catalog Number 93-090370
ISBN 1 - 883772 - 00 - 1

Printed by Bridgetown Printing, Portland, Oregon
Binding by Lincoln and Allen, Portland, Oregon
Color seperations by Imageworks Too Inc., Portland, Oregon
This book is printed on recycled paper using soy-based inks.

INTRODUCTION

As more and more people live on this planet, more and more of what we do affects the world's ecosystems. That isn't always good. We think of the oceans as large, untamed wildernesses, but in fact they are getting polluted. Often we manage ocean resources by what's good for us, not what's good for them. That means some animal populations are becoming badly damaged, and so are the habitats that are their homes.

What will it take to keep the oceans and their animals safe and healthy? It will take a new generation of dedicated scientists and teachers who want to protect and conserve what we've got. That means it will take you and your friends and classmates. And it will take organizations like the Oregon Coast Aquarium, which help people care about the world in which they live.

Allen Monroe
Director of Animal Husbandry and Life Support
Oregon Coast Aquarium

A PLACE OF WONDER

The Oregon Coast Aquarium is a private nonprofit, educational facility. The goal of the aquarium is to educate a broad spectrum of the public about the unique and abundant natural resources of the Oregon coast, so that they can be responsible stewards of those resources now and in the future.

Oregon Coast Aquarium
2820 S.E. Ferry Slip Road
Newport, Oregon 97365
(503) 867-3123

**This is the story of a small boy named Billy,
who thinks taking a bath is really quite silly.**

**"To sit in the tub is a waste of my time,
I'd much rather play in the dirt and the grime."**

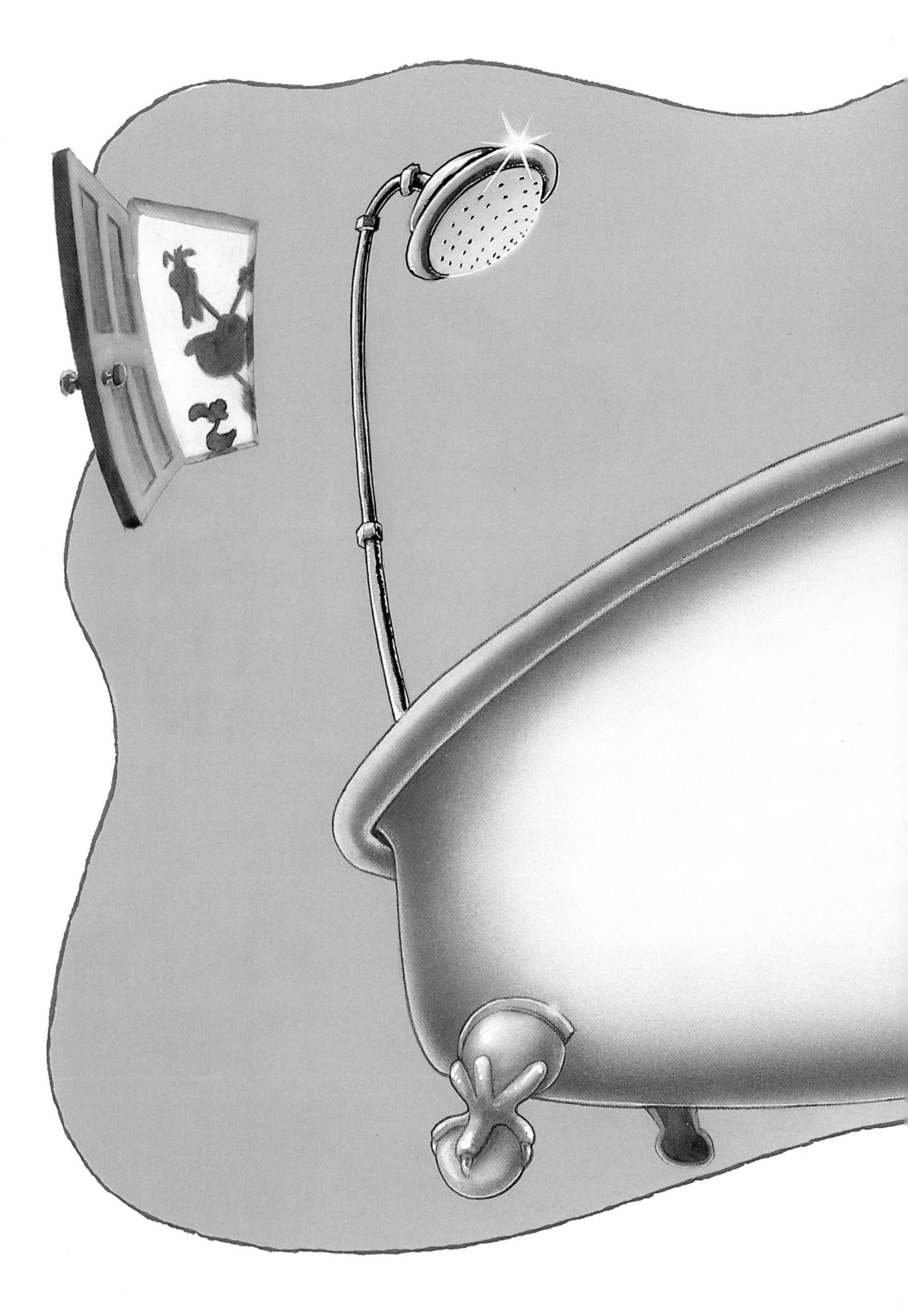

Billy's mom, on the other hand, thinks baths are a must…
she says it's important to clean off the crust.

**Soooo... every night Billy and Molly crawl in the tub,
for a fate worse than death, a good soapy scrub.**

**“No matter how hard I try, I get soap in my eye…
and my fingers and toes turn to prunes.**

I don't like taking baths… they make me very upset,
it's really quite simple—I hate getting wet!"

Billy finished his bath
and was about to get out,
when he noticed some bubbles
bubbling about.
A million small bubbles
bubbling about...
hiding the tip of a black
and white snout.

Billy's body went limp
and his dog turned quite
pale... because out of
the tub burst a huge
Orca whale.

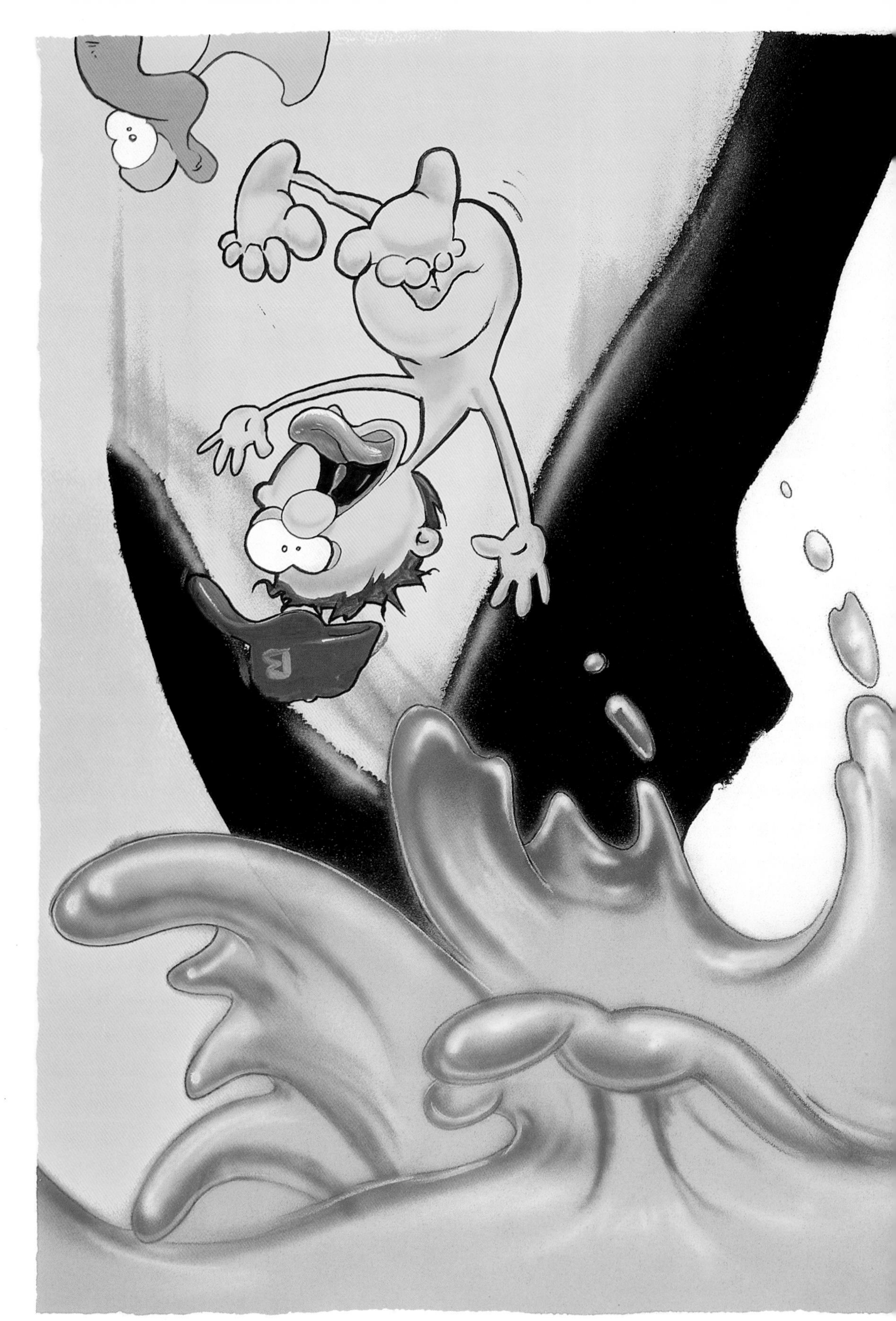

“I was just swimming by,” sang the whale, “when I heard what you said, and I cannot believe that it’s bathtime you dread.

So wipe the frown off your face and quit singing the blues;
it's time for this crew to take a magical cruise."

A brisk salty wind from the northeast did blow,
and the currents and waves then started to flow…

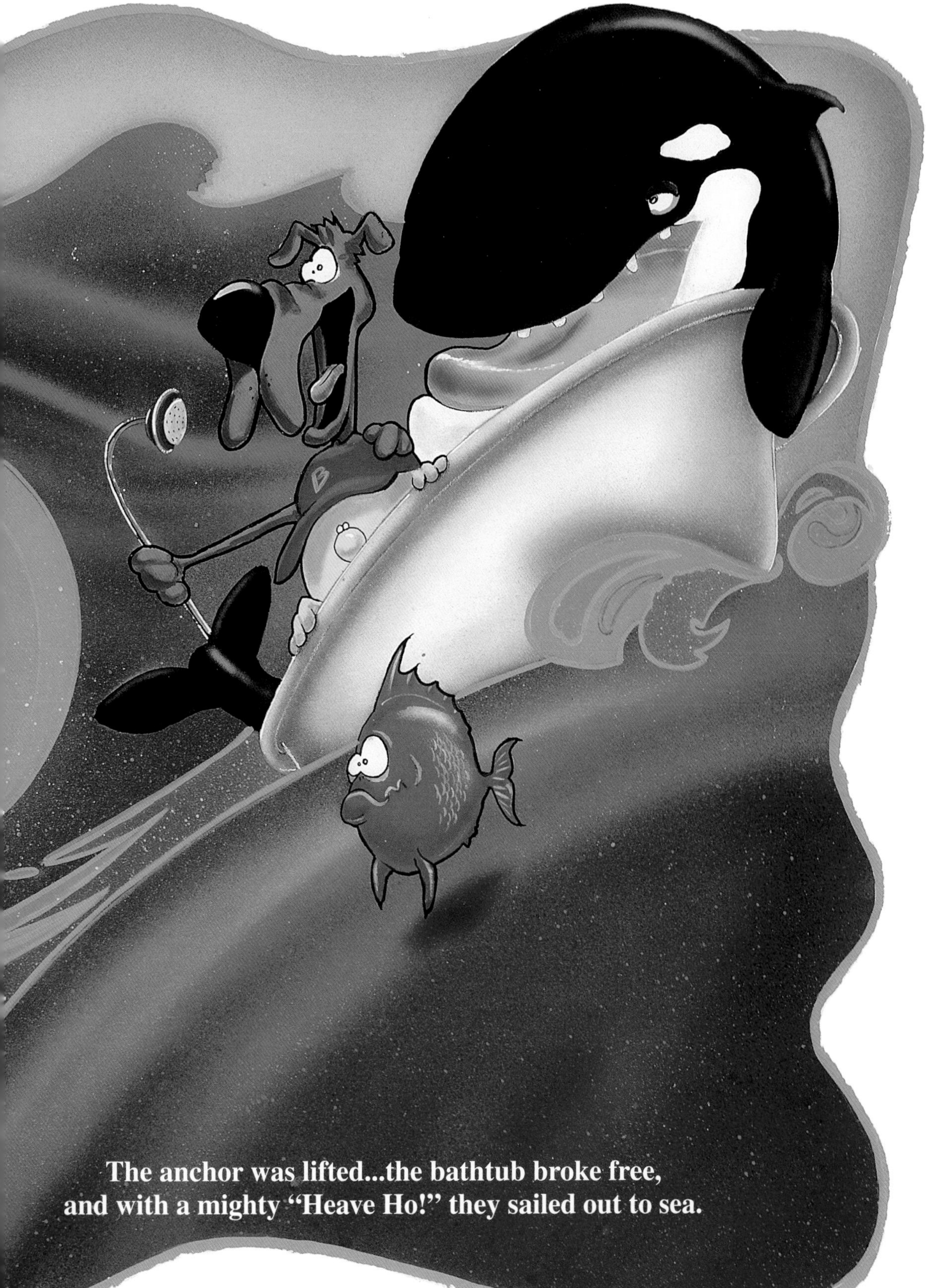

The anchor was lifted...the bathtub broke free,
and with a mighty "Heave Ho!" they sailed out to sea.

What is a fish?

A fish is a creature that is usually covered with scales, breathes with its gills and lives under water. All fish are vertebrates, which means that they have a backbone and internal skeleton.

"You see, said the whale, there are millions of fish taking baths all the time...

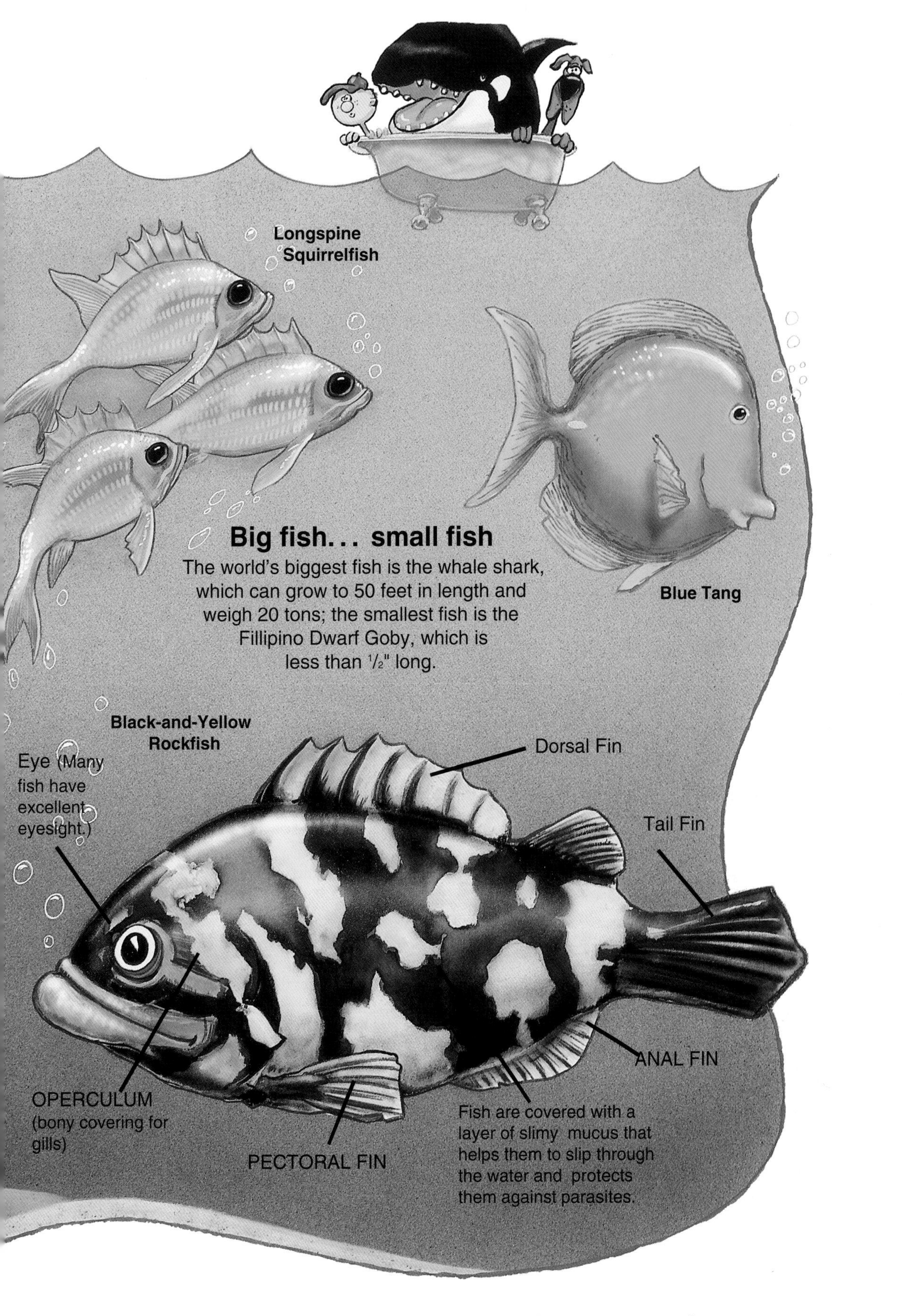

they're always quite clean... no dirt, dust or grime.

Take a deep breath...

Whales breathe air through a blowhole at the top of their heads. A blue whale can dive as deep as 1,500 feet and can stay under water for up to two hours at a time.

The spout of a whale, which isn't water but actually water vapor, can reach heights of 30 feet.

Bottlenose Dolphin

Whales travel in groups called pods!

Think about this...

Whales, dolphins and porpoise are considered some of the smartest creatures living in the ocean. The Sperm Whale has a brain that weighs close to 20 pounds, the largest brain of any animal.

Sperm Whale

All these creatures are happy... to the very last trout...

Do all whales have teeth?

NO! While all dolphins and porpoise have teeth, only some species of whales have teeth.There are two types of whales, the toothed whales and baleen whales. Baleen is a hard bone-like substance that acts like a giant filter. Dolphins, porpoise and toothed whales catch and eat their food one item at a time, while baleen whales filter entire schools of fish, squid and crustaceans.

Right Whale

What's for dinner?

The main course for many baleen whales consists of small shrimp-like creatures called krill. These krill swim in large groups called shoals. The whale will simply swim through the shoal of krill with its mouth open, forcing the water out and trapping the krill in the baleen filters. A blue whale may eat up to four tons of krill a day.

Krill

...so I can't understand what you're moaning about.

Go South, young whale...

Gray whales make one of the longest annual migrations of any animal on earth. These giant creatures journey 6,000 miles every year to get from their summer feeding grounds in the Arctic to their winter breeding waters in southern California. About 20,000 whales swim this journey, staying within two miles of the Pacific coastline. The entire migration takes about six to eight weeks.

Rock - a - bye baby...

Some baby whales weigh up to two tons and are 20 feet long at birth. These giant babies need to drink over 25 gallons of rich mother's milk a day to get the proper nutrition. At one year of age a young whale will weigh close to 30 tons.

Humpback Whale

Billy rolled his eyes and huffed,
"You big, goofy fish, are you completely insane?

The big and small of it.

The largest animal on earth is the blue whale. The blue whale can grow to be 100 feet in length and weigh as much as 90 to 95 tons. Not all members of the whale family are as big as the blue whale; the harbor porpoise can measure as small as four feet in length, weighing only 100 pounds.

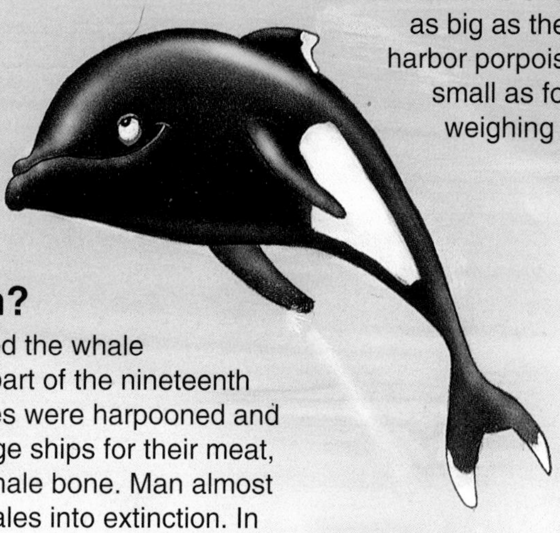

Dall's Porpoise

Extinction?

Man has hunted the whale since the last part of the nineteenth century. Whales were harpooned and pulled onto large ships for their meat, blubber and whale bone. Man almost hunted the whales into extinction. In 1987 commercial whaling was outlawed and today the whales are making a slow comeback. Some nations, however, still insist on hunting whales illegally.

What's the difference between fish and whales?

There are several major differences between fish and the group called cetacea (a scientific name for whales, dolphins and porpoise). All of these animals may be referred to as whales.

1. Whales, dolphins and porpoise are mammals.
2. Whales, dolphins and porpoise are air-breathing.
   (Fish breathe underwater with gills.)
3. Whales, dolphins and porpoise are warm-blooded.
4. Whales, dolphins and porpoise give birth to live young.

I think all of this water has gone straight to your brain!

No bones about it...

Sharks have no bones! The entire shark "skeleton" is made of cartilage, making the shark an extremely flexible creature.

Great White Shark

Smile...

Sharks have several rows of razor sharp teeth. As the front row of teeth is worn down or knocked out, it is replaced by a new row of teeth from the back of the mouth.

.......Roughing it!

A shark's skin is very tough and is covered with millions of small "teeth" called denticles. If you rub a shark's skin one way it will feel smooth; if you rub it the opposite way it will feel rough.

A bath may sound swell if you're a shark, bass or pike...

...but taking a bath is not what I like."

Horsing around...
The **seahorse** is a poor swimmer who relies on its ability to change colors like a chameleon to hide from predators and to sneak up on prey. These strange little fish feed by sucking tiny water creatures into their tube-shaped mouths. Their eyes can move independently, allowing them to watch for food as well as predators.

Mr. Mom...
During the seahorse breeding season the female seahorse will lay up to 200 eggs in the pouch located on the lower abdomen of the male. About two to five weeks later the eggs have developed into baby seahorses ready to be born.

Sea Horse

"First...let's get our facts straight," huffed the black and white orca, as he twitched his huge tail...

Manta rays seem to take flight under the water as they gracefully beat their pectoral fins much like a bird beats its wings. All Manta rays have cephalic fins on either side of their mouths to help funnel plankton and small fish into the filter feeding mouth. Manta rays can grow to a width of over 18 feet and a weight of 3,000 pounds.

Manta Ray

Jelly Fish

Moray Eels can be found swimming in snake-like fashion, but they usually spend their time under a ledge or in a hole along the coral. Their mouths are full of pointed teeth, yet they generally bite only when provoked.

Moray Eel

Sea Urchin

"I am hardly a fish but rather a whale!"

Way down deep...

Gone fishin'...

The black devil or anglerfish has a large light organ at the end of a long, thin fin. This fin is used as a fishing pole and the light at the end of the fin attracts small fish. When the smaller fish swims up to the light the anglerfish quickly swallows it up in its tooth-filled mouth.

Anglerfish

Oh say, can you see...

Because it is so dark in the depths of the ocean many fish have to provide their own light. These deep water fish have light organs (photophores) that provide a glowing light that enables them to attract and see prey as well as help find potential mates. The lights are made up of billions of glowing bacteria. About 1,500 species of deep sea fish can produce their own light.

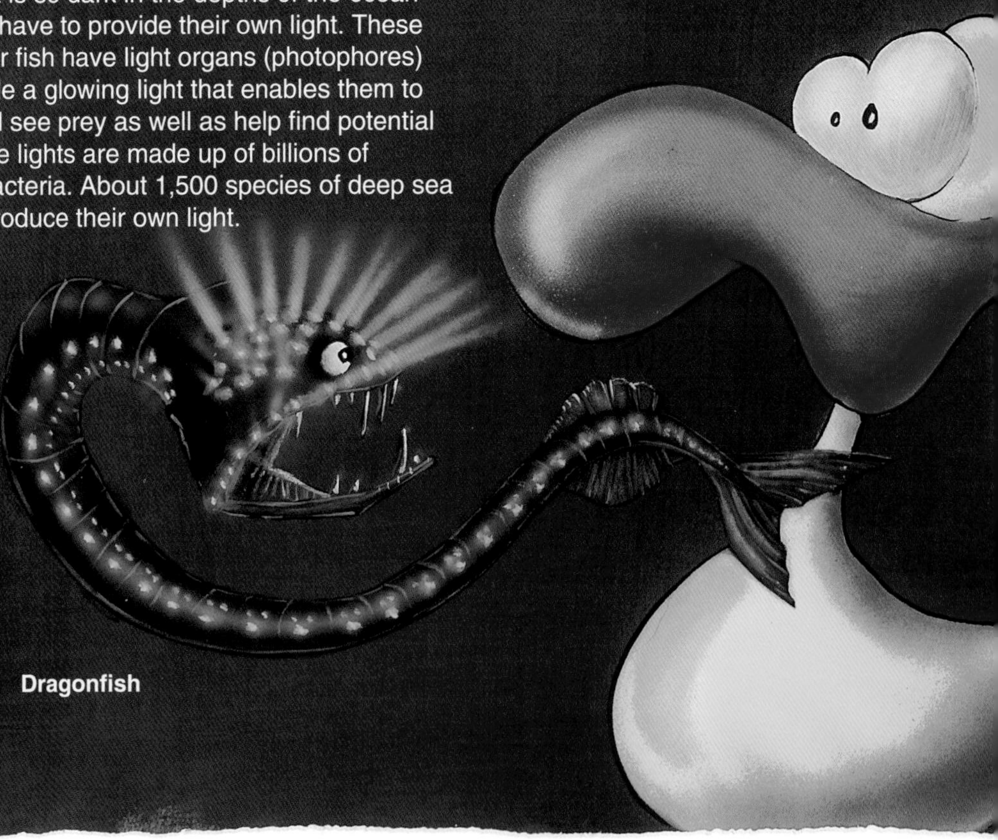

Dragonfish

Well you may be a whale, smirked Billy, but you're a whale who.. can't hear...

Hatchet fish!

Hatchet fish live several hundred feet below the surface. These strange fish have eyes that are turned upward and act like binoculars. These special eyes enable the hatchet fish to scan the water above for the silhouettes of small fish. The hatchet fish itself is very flat so that it doesn't make a silhouette that would attract predators from deeper down.

Hatchetfish

Deep sea fish are often small, colored black or brown and have long sharp teeth to insure prey they catch doesn't escape.

Pacific Viperfish

Catching prey in the ocean depths is very difficult. Since it may be weeks between meals, some deep sea fish have flexible stomachs that lets them eat as much as possible when a meal is caught.

...could it be that you have seaweed stuck in your ear?"

Sockeye Salmon

Incredible Journey...

Salmon begin their life in freshwater streams and rivers. After hatching, young salmon spend about two years in the freshwater environment before they migrate to the ocean. They live 2 or 3 years in the saltwater, getting fat to prepare for the spawning journey. The salmon must fight swift currents, fisherman, bears, waterfalls and dams to get to the exact spot where they were born so that they can spawn (lay eggs). When they get to the spawning grounds the females dig out nests 2 to 12 inches deep in the river or stream bed and then deposit the eggs. The male then fertilizes the eggs. After the salmon are done reproducing many of the adults die. The salmon carcasses decompose giving many valuable nutrients to the new generation of salmon that will be hatching. A female may lay 4,000 to 5,000 eggs. From all of those eggs, it is not unusual for only 3 or 4 to grow into adults and return to spawn.

Atlantic Wolffish

I'll tell you right now, Mr. Whale, for the very last time...

If looks could kill...

The lionfish is one of the most poisonous fish in the sea. This beautiful creature has glands at the end of its fins that contain a powerful venom. The venom can cripple predators and prove fatal to humans. The lionfish is about 15 inches long and lives along rocks and reefs in warm regions.

The top five "real but weird" fish names:

5.Jolthead Porgy
4. Greater Soapfish
3. Onespot Fringehead
2. Shortspine Thornyhead
1. Monkeyface Prickleback

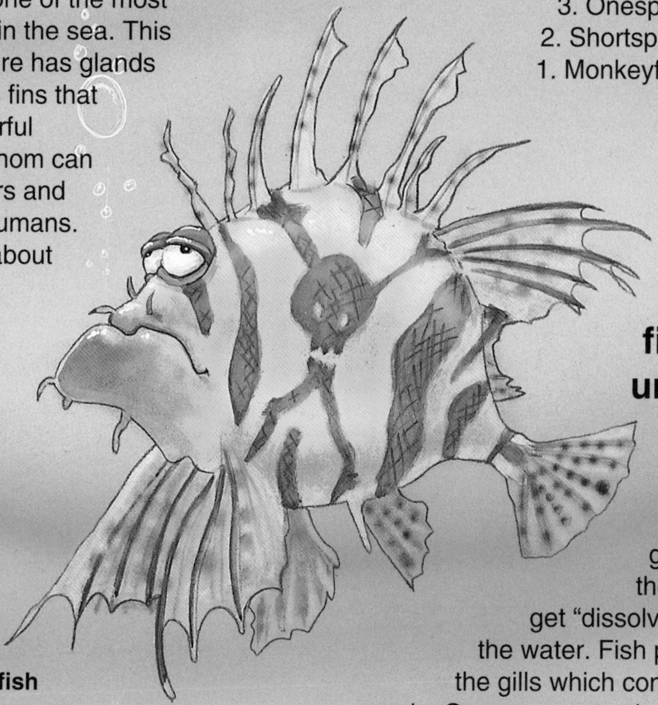

Lionfish

How do fish breathe underwater?

Fish need oxygen just like humans do. While a human gets oxygen from the air, a fish must get "dissolved" oxygen from the water. Fish pump water over the gills which contain a rich blood supply. Oxygen passes through the thin gill membranes directly into the fish's blood. The blood then distributes the oxygen throughout the fish's body.

I'll huff and puff...

Puffer fish are covered with spines.When they are cornered or threatened they can inflate to twice their normal size.

Porcupine Fish

I really enjoy the dirt, dust and grime."

Up, up and away...

The flying fish have very large fins that act as wings. These fins allow the fish to glide along the surface of the water, giving the impression of flight. These fish can glide at speeds close to 30 miles per hour when escaping predators.

Flying Fish

Eye eye captain...

There are over 5oo species of flatfish that live on the ocean floor. When these fish are born they are very similar to other fish... but some amazing changes take place as the fish gets older. In several weeks the fish's body becomes thin and flat and one of the eyes begins shifting over to the other side of the head until both eyes are on the same side.

Loggerhead

Hide and seek...

The flounder has mastered the art of camouflage. A flounder can become almost invisible by changing colors and patterns to match the sand or gravel on the ocean floor.

Flounder

The whale just whispered, "If you'll stop being such a stubborn boy, I'll show you the ways to make bathtime a joy.

Zoooom!

The marlin is the fastest hunter in the ocean. It can reach speeds of 60 miles per hour when it is chasing its prey.

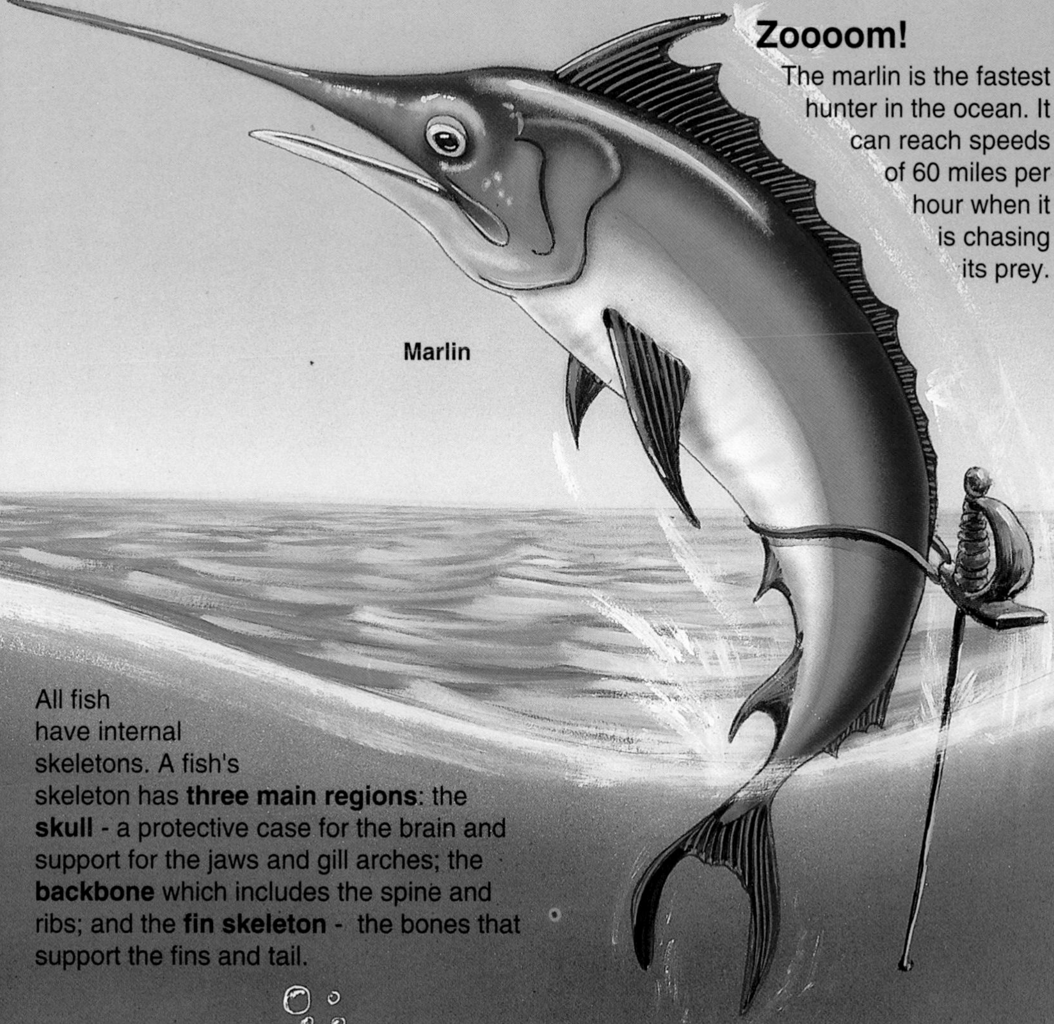

Marlin

All fish have internal skeletons. A fish's skeleton has **three main regions**: the **skull** - a protective case for the brain and support for the jaws and gill arches; the **backbone** which includes the spine and ribs; and the **fin skeleton** - the bones that support the fins and tail.

Some fish have skeletons that are **bone and cartilage**. These fish are known as **primitive bony fish**. (Sturgeon are examples of primitive bony fish.) Sharks and rays have skeletons made of **cartilage only**. These are called **cartilaginous fish**.

So listen real close -make a list if you wish-
of these great bathtime secrets shared by the fish!

Come out of your shell...

Like a child who outgrows his or her clothes, a crustacean grows out of its shell. Every year when a crab or lobster has outgrown its shell it will shed or molt the shell that is too small. Crustaceans also have the ability to discard a leg or claw that has been trapped or injured. There is a special point where the limb connects with the body that allows the limb to drop off with little bleeding. The limb will slowly grow back in stages every time the crustacean molts.

Purple Shore Crab

Oregon Cancer Crab

Red Crab

Horseshoe Crab

FIRST... Don't be alone when you sit in the tub...
round up some friends to help you to scrub."

Crustaceans

Crabs, lobsters and prawns are all examples of crustaceans. Crustaceans usually have antennae, jointed legs and a hard shell that protects their bodies. These creatures vary greatly in size. The smallest of the crustaceans are microscopic critters that are part of floating plankton; the largest are the giant spider crabs which can measure 12 feet across their claw tips.

Molly Dog

California Fiddler Crab

Australian Lobster

Molly, a toy boat, and your rubber duck, Bob are very good choices to help do the job.

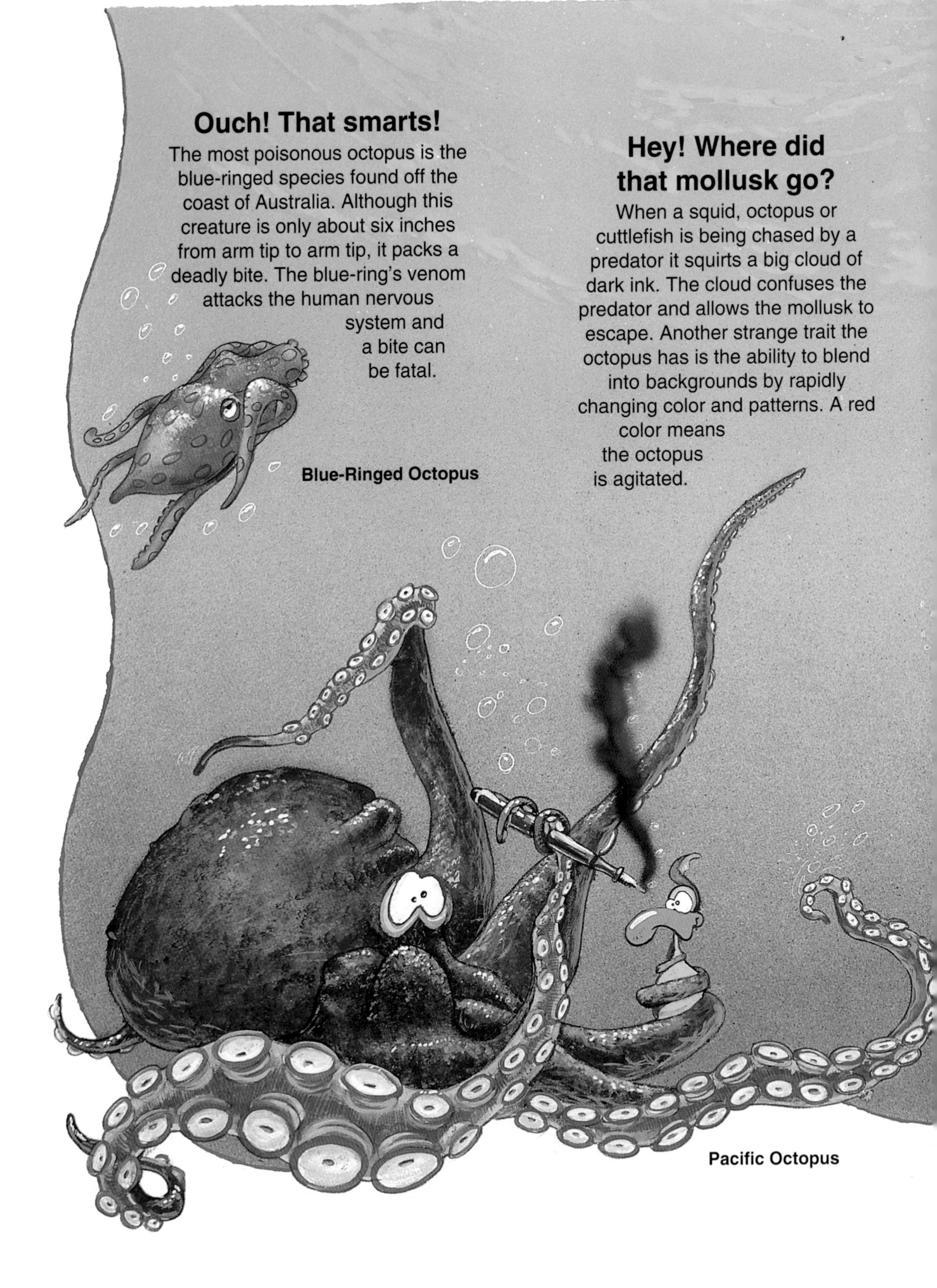

Ouch! That smarts!

The most poisonous octopus is the blue-ringed species found off the coast of Australia. Although this creature is only about six inches from arm tip to arm tip, it packs a deadly bite. The blue-ring's venom attacks the human nervous system and a bite can be fatal.

Blue-Ringed Octopus

Hey! Where did that mollusk go?

When a squid, octopus or cuttlefish is being chased by a predator it squirts a big cloud of dark ink. The cloud confuses the predator and allows the mollusk to escape. Another strange trait the octopus has is the ability to blend into backgrounds by rapidly changing color and patterns. A red color means the octopus is agitated.

Pacific Octopus

NEXT... while the water is running, avoid some of your troubles...

Mommy dearest...

The female octopus lays eggs only once in her life. When she is three years of age she will lay approximately 50,000 tiny eggs, usually hanging them on the roof of a small underwater cave. The female will spend the next six months spraying clean water on the eggs with nozzle-like spouts located on the side of her head. Soon after the young hatch the mother will die. The male dies soon after he fertilizes the eggs.

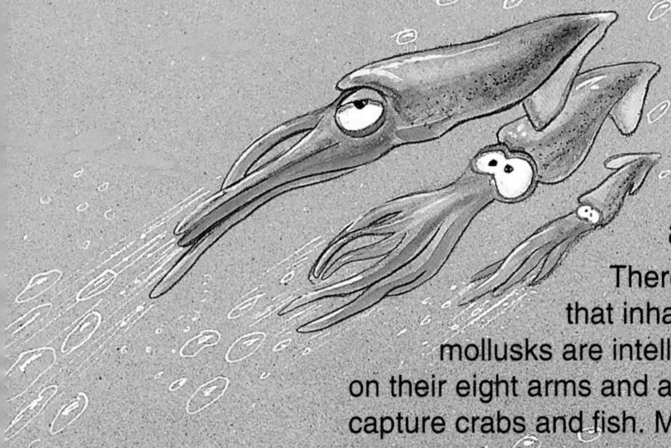

Giant Squid...

The giant squid is the world's largest invertebrate (animal without a backbone). These squid can grow to be more than 50 feet in length and weigh up to two tons.

Arm in arm in arm in arm in arm in arm in arm in arm...

There are over 150 species of octopus that inhabit the earth's oceans. These mollusks are intelligent creatures that use the suckers on their eight arms and a rock-hard beak to hunt and capture crabs and fish. Most of these octopi live in warm tropical waters, yet the largest ones are located in the North Pacific Ocean. The world's largest octopus had tentacles spanning over 23 feet in length and weighed over 118 pounds.

Squid are the fastest mollusk... reaching speeds of 20 mph.

Common Octopus

...make bathtime exciting and dump in some bubbles!"

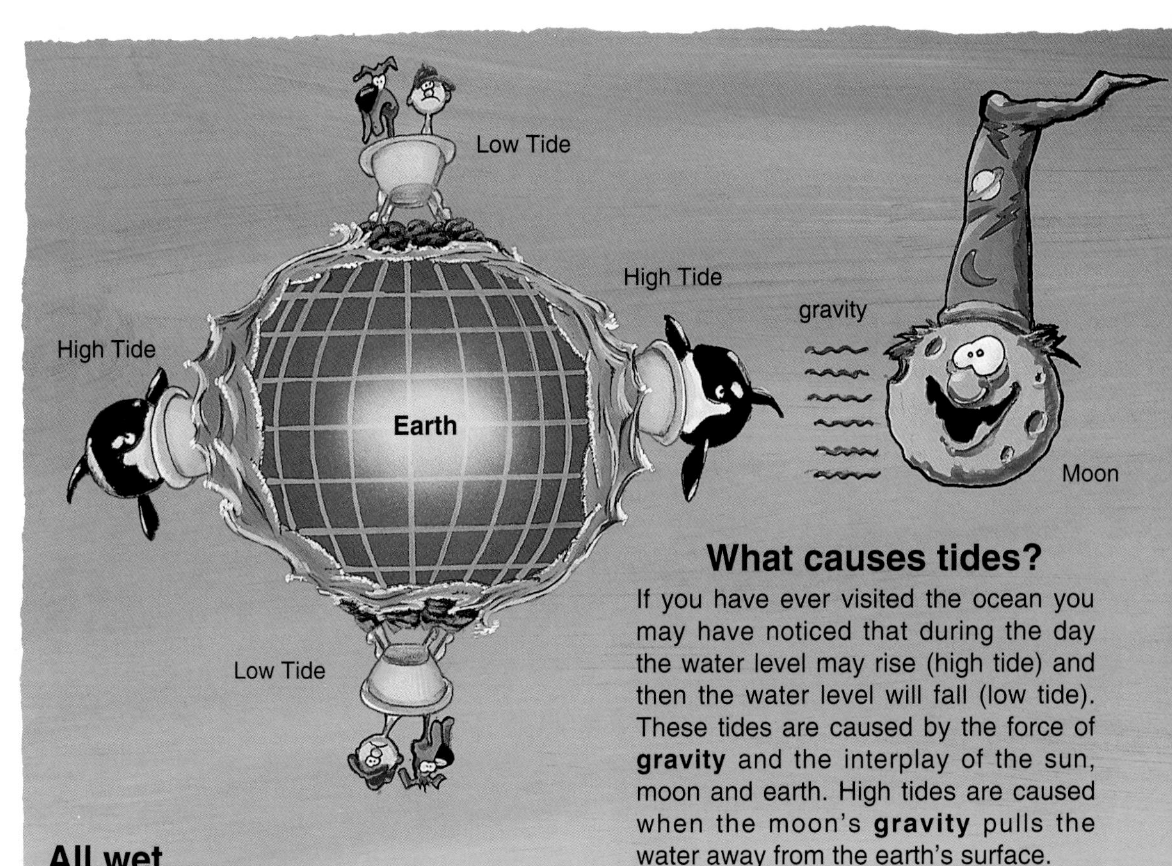

What causes tides?

If you have ever visited the ocean you may have noticed that during the day the water level may rise (high tide) and then the water level will fall (low tide). These tides are caused by the force of **gravity** and the interplay of the sun, moon and earth. High tides are caused when the moon's **gravity** pulls the water away from the earth's surface.

All wet...

The ocean is a huge body of salt water that covers three-quarters of the earth.

More on tides...

There are actually two high tides happening at the same time on earth. The side closest to the moon has a high tide but so does the side farthest from the moon. Just as the moon pulls the water from the earth on the close side the moon is also pulling the earth away from the water on the opposite side.

A mountain of bubbles may seem kind of weird...

Gravity is an attraction between two masses; the **gravitational pull** is determined by how big the two objects are and the distance between them.

Why are high tides higher during different parts of the month?

At certain times during the month the moon and sun line up in such a way that their **gravitational pulls** reinforce each other. When this happens the stronger gravitational pull causes high tides or "spring tides" (spring tides don't necessarily happen in the spring). When the moon and sun are out of alignment and their gravitational pulls are working against each other the high tides are lower; these tides are called "neap tides."

...but when wiped on your chin it makes a soap bubble beard.

Sea Anemone

The **Hermit Crab** lives in empty shells of mollusks. When the crab grows too big for the shell it looks for another larger shell to move into.

Sea stars have the strange ability to grow a new arm if on is cut off. This is known as **regeneration**. In some cases if a sea star is cut completely in half the entire missing half may regenerate.

Limpets

Hang in there...

Once a Limpets has grasped a rock with its muscular foot it is very difficult to pry it off. Each limpet has a "home base" where it has dug a shallow pit in a rock with its shell.

You see, said the whale, "the secret for fish, beast and child...

Mussel Bound...

Mussels attach..... themselves to the rocky shore with tough threads called byssus.

On the right foot...

Sea stars and sea urchins have hundreds of tiny tube feet while limpets and sea snails have a single suction foot.

Scallops

Sanddollar

Sea urchin...

The sea urchin is protected by sharp spines. It uses hundreds of tube- like feet to anchor and drag itself along the rocks. It will scavenge for bits of food, as well as, graze on seaweeds.

Sea urchin

Trash Man...

Many crabs are very good scavengers. They pick up almost anything that's edible from the ocean floor.

Prawn

Mountain Crab

...is to make bathtime an adventure, let your imagination go wild!

What are pinnipeds?

Seals, sea lions and walruses all belong to the pinniped family. There are over 30 species of pinnipeds that inhabit every ocean in the world. Pinnipeds are comfortable both on land and in the water. These creatures are excellent swimmers and divers; they can dive as deep as half a mile to capture their prey. Even though pinnipeds breathe air they can stay under water for 20 to 30 minutes. A thick layer of blubber protects them from the frigid waters they may encounter.

Seal you later...

The California sea-lion is one of the fastest pinnipeds, traveling at speeds over 20 miles per hour.

Southern Elephant Seal

The **southern elephant seal** is the largest species in the pinniped family. The adult male can reach a weight of 6,000 pounds. These mammoth creatures live in the icy Antarctic waters and can be recognized by their large noses. These animals also vocalize by using a series of gargles, burps and whines.

Otters

Sea Otter

Sea otters rarely come to shore, spending much of their time relaxing in the middle of a kelp bed. (Sometimes otters will actually wrap themselves in kelp so they won't float away while napping.) Otters will often use a rock to break open the shell of a sea urchin, crab or other prey.

Maybe, one night, you'll become a pirate searching for treasure... or hunting a serpent too long to measure."

Nice mustache...

A walrus has about 700 hairs on its nose. These hairs are about 35 times thicker than human hair. These whiskers are used to search for shellfish.

Harbor Seal

Walrus

Billy sat up and yelled, "I see what you mean. I could be the captain of a green submarine, on a top secret mission to get my toes clean!"

Rock sweet home...
A large number of sea birds nest along coastal cliffs and rocky islands that can only be reached by flight. This makes these locations very safe for the birds and keeps them close to the shore where they can hunt for food.

The puffin will sometimes catch up to ten fish on one dive. It will line the fish up in its bill and take them back to the nest

Great white pelican...
The pelican has a beak adapted for hunting fish. The bottom of the beak is actually a large pouch. When the pelican dips its bill in the water the pouch expands filling with water and small fish. As the bird lifts its head the pouch contracts expelling the water and trapping the fish. Sometimes a group of five to ten pelicans will stand in a horseshoe shape to hunt together. They dip their bills together causing a large circle of open pouches trapping most of the fish in that area.

Great White Pelican

Whimbrel

Common Puffin

The whale made some sense...Billy's heart had been won, this bathtime thing might even be fun.

Put it on my bill...

Many birds that live near the ocean eat fish. These fish are slimy and slippery and tend to jump and wiggle quite a bit. Ocean birds have bills or beaks that are made just for catching and hanging on to fish. Gulls and cormorants, for example, have a hook or curved tip on their beaks that keeps the fish from slipping out of the end. Some birds have beaks designed to hammer or peck open crab shells and other birds have beaks that work as spears. The gannet dives from as high as 100 feet to spear and catch small fish.

Albatross

Emperor penquins nest in Antarctica in the middle of winter while temperatures are reaching -70 degrees. The female lays a single egg. It is then up to the male to take care of the egg. The male will balance the egg up on his feet to keep it from getting too cold, sometimes not eating or moving around for nine weeks. When the egg hatches the female returns to feed and care for the chick.

It's a bird... it's a plane...

Some ocean birds have white or light colored undersides so that they will blend in with the clouds and make them less visible to prey living below.

MAP

ANTARCTICA

Red-throated Loon

Emperor Penquin

Gala'pagos Penquin

**Billy hugged his Great Dane and gave a loud cheer,
"I think that I'll bathe more than three times a year!"**

The little white tub started for home...
leaving behind the soft ocean foam.

“Land Ho,” yelled the orca, giving his crew a small wink,
"I think we’ll drop anchor by the ol’ bathroom sink."

Billy shook the whale's fin and said with a grin,
"This was a wonderful night, I've had a real ball...

...But you guys better shove off, I hear my mom down the hall!"

The bathroom door opened to reveal Billy's mother. She gave him a glare and then gave him another. "You've been awfully quiet, young man... are you causing some scene?" Billy giggled, "No, dearest mother... I'm just getting clean."

She smiled a small smile and disappeared down the hall, not even noticing the sea star stuck on the wall.

ABOUT THE AUTHORS

RAY NELSON is a very big person (six feet four inches tall) and has always loved to draw strange characters and write silly stories. He was always drawing. He drew on homework...he drew on walls and he drew on his little brother, Troy. Ray spent five years as an animator and designer for Will Vinton Studios in Portland, Oregon before starting his own business, Flying Rhino Productions. Besides writing and illustrating, Ray also speaks to thousands of school children about cartooning and the importance of persistance, self-esteem and confidence. Today Ray spends most of his time entertaining his new daughter Alexandria, entertaining his wife Theresa, or just trying to stay out of trouble. (Occasionally he might be found cleaning up the hair and drool that has been scattered about his house by Molly the great dane.)

DOUGLAS KELLY is a very nice man. He has a fuzzy beard and isn't very tall. (He reminds Ray of a hamster.) Doug has spent the last few years as a set designer for Will Vinton Studios in Portland, Oregon. He learned how to be an artist by watching his father (who is also an artist), and studying real hard at Mt. Hood Community College and The Art Center of Design in Pasadena , California. Doug would like to thank the Academy, his agent and all the little people that he stepped on to win this award. (When informed that he actually hasn't won anything...and that this is an informational paragraph about his personal life, Doug seemed very disappointed.) Doug enjoys golfing, saving cats from the tops of very tall trees, spending time with Victoria and creating world peace.

ACKNOWLEDGMENTS

A SPECIAL THANK YOU TO OUR VERY GOOD FRIENDS

Gene Kelly, Ray and Chris Nelson Sr., Edna Nelson, Theresa Nelson, Harbormaster, **Victoria Collins,** crustacean wrangler, **Mike and Holly McLane,** explosives experts, **Kevin Atkinson,** Billy's stunt double, **Ben Adams,** assistant to Molly Dog, **Susan Ring,** Tuna Tuner, **Jacelen Pete,** Bob, the rubber duck's stunt double, **Shaunna Griggs,** Rubber Duck Trainer, **Mark Hansen,** Fish Wrangler, **Troy Nelson,** Pinniped Choreographer, **Alexandria Nelson,** Drool consultant, **Deborah Beilman,** Mollusk costumes. **Kelly Kuntz,** and all of the wonderful kids at Hiteon Elementary School in Beaverton Oregon.

This project would never have set sail if it weren't for the contribution of these wonderful individuals. Thank you !

FLYING RHINO PRODUCTIONS

Flying Rhino Productions is a company that believes in educating the children of the world. While we create and produce our books, animation, music and clothes, education is the number one priority. If for any reason you are unhappy with a Flying Rhino product you may return it for a full refund. Comments are appreciated.

To get a free brochure about books and clothes call,
1 - 800 - Le RHINO
1 - 800 - 537 - 4466

Other Flying Rhino Books
The Incredible Adventures of Donovan Willoughby
The Internal Adventures of Donovan Willoughby
(Health and Anatomy)
Greetings from America
(American Geography)
Connie and Bonnie's Birthday Blastoff
(Space)
A Dinosaur Ate My Homework
(Dinosaurs)

Flying Rhino Productions 3629 SW Caldew Portland, Oregon 97219